ADVENTURES IN FRONTIER AMERICA

LOG-CABIN HOME

Pioneers in the Wilderness

by Catherine E. Chambers

Illustrated by Allan Eitzen

Troll Associates

Library of Congress Cataloging in Publication Data

Chambers, Catherine E.
   Log-cabin home.

   (Adventures in frontier America)
   Summary: In 1802 the Craley family set up a new home
in Kentucky where they hope to find good land for
farming.
   [1. Frontier and pioneer life—Kentucky—Fiction]
I. Eitzen, Allan, ill. II. Title. III. Series: Chambers,
Catherine E. Adventures in frontier America.
PZ7.C3558Lo 1984   [Fic]   83-18277
ISBN 0-8167-0041-9
ISBN 0-8167-0042-7 (pbk.)

LOG-CABIN HOME

Pioneers in the Wilderness

Matt Craley whistled as he walked through the woods. His dog Red frisked around him. Matt was twelve years old, and he thought being a pioneer was exciting. Today Pa was letting him lead the way. Red ran ahead, sniffing at animal tracks in the underbrush.

Not far behind Matt came Pa, his long Kentucky rifle under his arm. Pa looked just like a woodsman should, in his coarse linen hunting shirt and the fine fringed buckskin britches he had made. On his feet were shoepacks, which looked like moccasins but with sturdy soles and high tops that tied round his legs. Matt went barefoot. So did his younger sister Becky. Ma rode on old Nellie, the mare, with bundles piled behind her. The family's iron cooking pot sat on top of the bundles, looking like the top of a throne behind Ma's head. Ma held a rope to lead Blaze, their other horse. Blaze wore a loaded packsaddle. In it were an axe, a hoe, sacks of food and seed, a skillet, wooden plates, and Ma's prized pewter mug. Roped to Blaze was Hester the cow. Even Hester had a pack to carry. The year was 1802. The Craleys were moving through the Cumberland Gap, a pass in the Cumberland Mountains bordering Kentucky. They were on their way to make a new home in Kentucky.

5

This was how most families traveled to the land beyond the mountains. Sometimes a young couple didn't even have animals to help them. Some people were "greenhorns"—that meant they didn't know the ways of the wilderness. But Pa was a good woodsman. He had grown up in the foothills of the Appalachian Mountains in Virginia. He had been through the Gap with the Continental Army. Now he was taking his family along that same route.

The wilderness was like a green cave, closed in with endless tree trunks. Few rays of sun came through the branches overhead. It was so lonely and silent. But Matt soon learned to like it. After two days, he began to listen for the *rat-tat-tat* of woodpeckers. He heard the faint *swish* as a snake slithered through the leaves. He caught glimpses of deer, although not as often as he had expected, for deer liked to graze on grass, not forest leaves. But there were opossum and woodchucks and squirrels. After he learned to spot the forest animals, Matt wasn't lonely any more.

Pioneers traveled slowly. They had to stop often to let the animals graze on leaves and shrubs. Before dark came

each night, Pa found a clearing where it was safe to make a
fire. Matt helped Pa unload the animals and tie them up,
so they could not stray. Becky was sent to gather wood.
Matt lit the fire by rubbing flint and steel together till a
spark flared. Ma brought water from a stream and put the
long-handled skillet on the fire. Sometimes they had only
johnnycake to eat, made of corn meal and water. Sometimes Pa or Matt shot a squirrel for Ma to cook.

At night they slept on the ground. Matt was glad it was spring, and the air was warm. Ma had the bundle of blankets for her bed, but Matt and Becky lay on the slippery carpet of pine needles. Matt liked their cool fresh scent. Red cuddled close to the children. Pa dozed sitting against a tree, his rifle on his knees. "I like to keep one eye

8

open against trouble," he always said. Sometimes at night Matt would gaze up at the tall trees. Some had trunks five or six feet thick and rose more than a hundred feet above the campers' heads.

"I hope we find trees like this to build with," Ma said. "That pine you slept against last night would have made a real fine table." Matt knew his mother felt sad about the furniture she had left behind. Pa and Matt had promised they would build her a good table and a cupboard, too. But more important things had to come first.

The mountains rose high on either side of the twisting trail. Becky stubbed her toe on a rock. "Ouch!" she cried. Matt looked at her.

"Are you all right?" he asked. She answered him with a grin with one tooth missing. Her sunbonnet was crooked, as usual, and there was mud on her face. In fact, they all were muddy from yesterday's rain.

"Cheer up," Pa told them. "We're almost to the Gap."

The trail was downhill now. The trees were not so thick here. Sunlight came through them, golden warm. They went round a sharp curve, and Pa said, "Look!"

9

They had come to the Cumberland Gap. On either side, trees marched upward in a crazy quilt of greens. To their left the trail dropped off to a gurgling stream. Red ran down and began to drink happily. Ahead, the trail wound between the mountains that met the sky in a blue smoky haze. Far beyond lay a valley, shimmering green and gold.

"That's where we're going," Pa said. "That's Kentucky."

Becky slid down to meet Red and dangled her feet in the clear water.

"Can we stop?" Ma asked longingly. "Nellie's tired. It's a warm day. And that stream looks good."

Pa grinned. "Guess we all could use some washing," he said.

They washed and splashed in the stream.

"I wish I could wash some clothes," Ma said. "I guess that has to wait till we get where we're going. How much farther is it, Joshua?"

"We'll know it when we get there" was all Pa would say.

Just any land in Kentucky wouldn't do, Matt knew. They wanted to be in the Ohio Valley, not the mountains. They needed land that they could farm. That meant it had to be fairly flat. The soil had to be good for crops. Pa would know that from the kind of trees that grew nearby. They needed to be near water. And they hoped there would be neighbors less than a day's ride away. "And sunlight," Ma said firmly. "We need a whole lot of sunlight."

The Craleys traveled for two more days. On the morning of the third day, Becky jumped up and down. "Smoke! I see smoke!"

"Where?" Pa jumped up quickly. Fire in the woods was very dangerous.

"I mean from a *people* fire," Becky said importantly. Down in the valley, a thin plume of smoke rose from a chimney.

"Neighbors," Ma said with joy.

Everybody was in a hurry that day. When the sun was about halfway down the western sky, they saw a cabin ahead of them in a clearing. A yellow dog ran out. He and Red sniffed noses, their tails waving.

A boy Matt's age came round the corner of the cabin. He stopped, stared, and ran back for a tall man. The dogs started barking. A woman and two little girls came from inside the cabin. The man came forward, smiling broadly, and holding out his hands to Pa. "Welcome! We're the Birkins. You must stay with us tonight."

It was wonderful being with people in a real home again. It was wonderful eating a real meal—venison stew, with vegetables from Mrs. Birkins' garden, and corn bread! Afterwards Matt and young Jake Birkins tended to the animals, and Becky helped her new friend Sarah Jane milk the cows. Then they all sat around the fire and talked. Pa told Mr. Birkins about their trip.

13

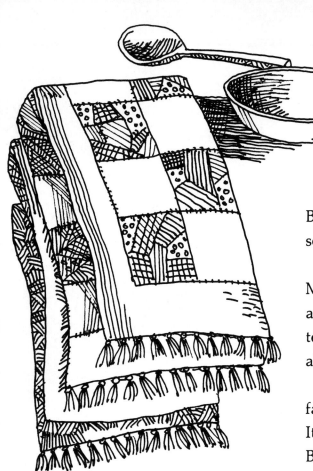

"You'll find very good farm land around here," Mr. Birkins said. "There are other families not far away. If you settle near, we'll all help you raise your cabin."

"It would be grand to have another family close by," Mrs. Birkins said. She showed Ma the quilts she'd made and the dishes Jake had whittled for her. Jake promised to teach Matt how to make some, too. Ma told Mrs. Birkins about the furniture she'd left behind.

That night Matt slept outside with Jake in the half-faced camp the Birkins had lived in when they first came. It was a shelter built into a hill, and it had an open side. Becky slept in the cabin loft with Sarah Jane and Emily. Pa and Ma slept in the Birkins' bed.

"You've slept on the ground every night since you left home. You'll do it again till you get your cabin raised. Tonight you have a bed with a real cornhusk mattress," Mrs. Birkins said. She and Mr. Birkins slept on blankets before the fire.

They all got up at dawn. The Birkins urged the Craleys to stay longer. But Ma and Pa were eager to find their own piece of land. So they loaded Nellie and Blaze and Hester and set out. There were no more steep mountains now. The trail led through a friendly valley. "When will we get there?" Becky kept asking. Pa kept saying, "You'll know. You'll know."

In the afternoon they came out of the woods into a little clearing. A stream gurgled to their right. Violets and dogwood trees were blooming. A squirrel ran, chattering, down a tree trunk. A mockingbird was singing cheerily.

Ma's eyes grew very bright. Becky jumped up and down. "I know! I know! We're here, aren't we, Pa?"

Pa turned to Matt. "What do you say, son? Does it look like good farming land?"

Matt's chest swelled. He scooped up a handful of earth and saw that it was good heavy soil. The roots of the native grass went deep. And there were not many stones that would cause trouble plowing. He saw that the trees had trunks the thickness of the logs in the Birkins' cabin. They were not so broad across that a man and boy together could not fell them.

"I think this looks very good," Matt said, grinning.

Ma slid down from Nellie and began to undo the harness. They were home.

The very next morning, Pa and Matt began to make a half-faced camp. First, they cut down trees. Then Pa found two forked tree trunks and set them up about ten feet apart. Everyone helped scoop out a hollow in the hill behind them. Pa put a pole between the two trunks, resting it in the forks. Ma and Becky helped take branches off logs that Pa and Matt stacked to make side walls. Then Pa laid light logs across the top to make a roof. Ma and Becky spread bark across the roof to help keep out rain. Pa built a campfire in front of the half-faced camp's open side. Matt made a frame from which Ma could hang her cooking pot over the fire.

"This will be fine for summer," Pa said. "But we'll have to raise our cabin before cold weather comes."

First, they had to clear land for farming and plant some crops. Pa picked a spot that would get a lot of sun. The smaller trees he and Matt cut down right away. The larger trees they girdled. This meant that they cut through the bark with the ax, all the way around the trunk. In time, the tree would die. Then it would be easier to take down.

While Pa and Matt cleared forest, Ma worked in the open space with the hoe. Where tree trunks stood, she made holes in the earth with the hoe handle. Becky walked behind her, dropping corn seed into the holes. Every few days, Pa went hunting. Sometimes he let Matt take the rifle and go without him. Matt became a very good shot. But he had to make sure not to get so far off in the woods that he couldn't find his way back. Once Becky did get lost, playing hide-and-seek with Red. After that, Ma put a bell around Becky's neck, and Matt made trail marks on the trees for a mile around.

One day Red started barking wildly. Matt looked up and saw two horses coming through the trees. The Birkins had come to visit!

Ma was glad Pa had shot a deer the day before. She was able to give the Birkins a real feast—venison, the first crop of corn, and berries Becky had gathered in the woods!

Jake showed Matt how to whittle wooden plates for Ma. Mrs. Birkins showed Ma how to plant seeds without all the work of hoeing uncleared land. She made gashes in

18

the earth with the ax and dropped the seeds into the cuts. Then she gave Ma some vegetable seeds from her own garden.

"When are you going to raise your cabin?" Mr. Birkins asked.

"I reckon September," Pa said. He was keeping track of the days and months by making notches in the wall of the half-faced camp.

By September a good plot of land had been cleared. The Craleys had harvested several crops of corn. Becky learned to scrape kernels off the ears with a knife. Ma gritted some ears of corn by rubbing them over the ax blade to make coarse corn meal. She hung vegetables and herbs to dry for winter use.

Pa and Matt cut trees for the cabin. Pa showed Matt the kind needed, about ten inches thick. Soon Matt was able to pick and cut many on his own. One day Pa found they had eighty tree trunks ready. He looked at Matt. "How'd you like to take Blaze tomorrow and ride over to the Birkins' cabin? You can tell them the Craleys are ready for their house-raising."

The house-raising was a three-day get-together for all the neighbors. The day before, Ma sent Matt out hunting. She made Becky sweep the half-face with a broom made from branches. Ma cooked all day. She wanted to be ready to welcome their new neighbors properly.

Early the first morning, folks started to arrive. Those who lived farthest had made half the journey the day before and spent the night with friends who lived closer to the Craleys. Some folks came in wagons. Some came on horseback, with their children walking. They brought their own knives and axes. They brought bedrolls to sleep on. They brought food. Ma's eyes were bright and her face pink from rushing around.

The first thing that happened was deciding where the cabin should stand. "Sunlight," Ma kept saying. "Lots of sunlight."

"Facing south," everybody told Pa. "That way you won't feel the worst of the winter winds."

Pa picked out a clearing close to the stream and facing south. He marked the layout of the house on the earth with his ax. Then men set to work cutting logs from the

trees that Pa and Matt had cut down. Horses dragged the logs into place. Two big logs ran the length of the cabin as a foundation. "Someday I'll make you a real wooden floor," Pa promised Ma. But for now the floor was just of hard-packed earth. The cabin would have one big room, sixteen by twenty feet.

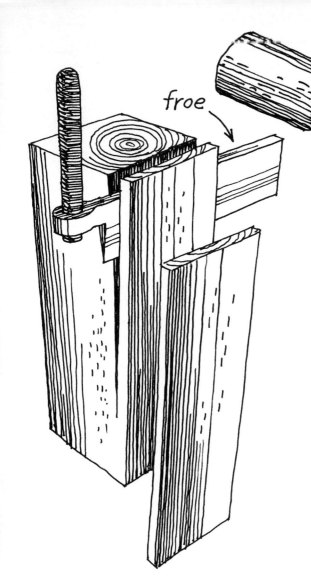

froe

club

Today the men and the older boys divided into three groups. One group dragged the logs into place. Another group settled the foundation firmly. The third group split clapboards for the roof. This was called "riving" and took great skill. The men cut logs three feet long and stood them on end. Then they split slabs from them with a froe. That was a long wedge-shaped blade with a handle sticking up from a socket at one end. First the blade was rested across the log. Then the blade was banged down into the log with a wooden club. This split the logs into planks about an inch thick.

After the day's work was done, everyone gathered around the fire. Food was passed around. People played games and sang. Some of the men danced wild dances. Matt was surprised when Pa showed them a jig he had learned on the trail with the Continental Army.

On the second day, most of the hardest work was done. A skilled man stood at each corner of the cabin. Then the others "rolled up" the walls. The corner men cut saddle-shaped notches a third of the way through each side of the logs. They used a piece of hide to measure the

distance between notches. If the notches were not just right, the walls would be crooked or have cracks open to the wind.

The cabin grew slowly, a log on each long side, then a log on each end. The notches locked the logs into one another. When the walls were too high for the men to lift logs onto them, Pa and Mr. Birkins leaned logs against the walls at an easy slope. Then the wall logs were rolled up the slanting logs and into place. When the walls were just higher than Pa's head, eight logs were laid across one end of the cabin. They supported the floor of the sleeping loft. Then a few more feet of walls were built up.

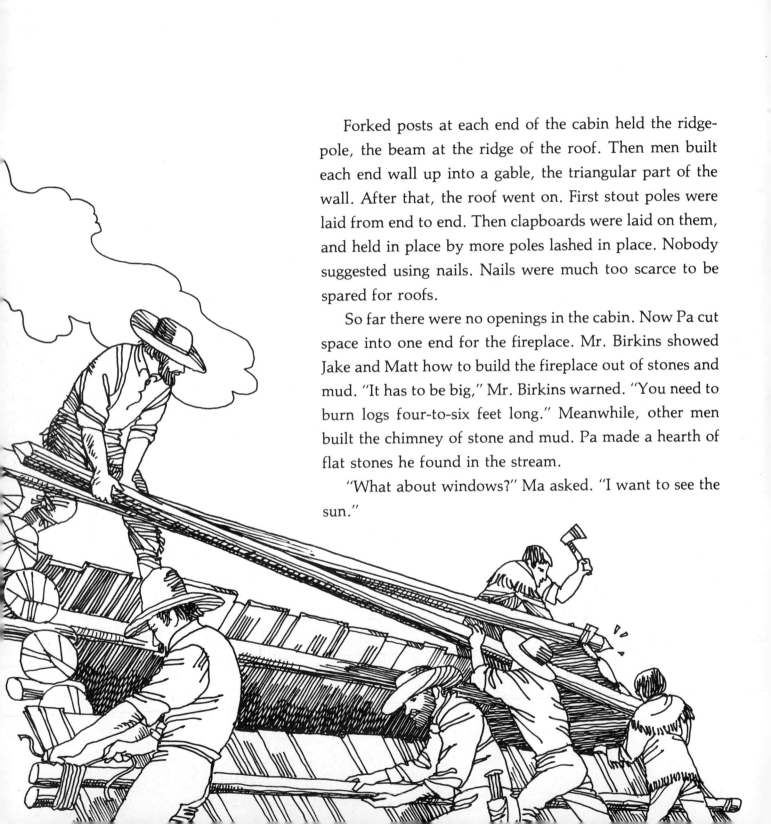

Forked posts at each end of the cabin held the ridge-pole, the beam at the ridge of the roof. Then men built each end wall up into a gable, the triangular part of the wall. After that, the roof went on. First stout poles were laid from end to end. Then clapboards were laid on them, and held in place by more poles lashed in place. Nobody suggested using nails. Nails were much too scarce to be spared for roofs.

So far there were no openings in the cabin. Now Pa cut space into one end for the fireplace. Mr. Birkins showed Jake and Matt how to build the fireplace out of stones and mud. "It has to be big," Mr. Birkins warned. "You need to burn logs four-to-six feet long." Meanwhile, other men built the chimney of stone and mud. Pa made a hearth of flat stones he found in the stream.

"What about windows?" Ma asked. "I want to see the sun."

The men shook their heads. Windows were a bad idea. Glass was much too breakable to bring through the mountains. Without glass, windows would be just open spaces to let in rain and cold. "And animals," Pa said. He knew that would make Ma think twice.

"I've heard of windows made of oiled silk or parchment," Ma said stubbornly.

"Maybe later," Pa said.

Before work stopped for the night, Pa cut a doorway.

The third day was the day for folks with special skills. The best craftsmen rived and polished planks to frame the doorway. They "nailed" them in place with wooden nails driven into holes that had been drilled into the planks. Jake knew how to whittle the nails, and he taught Matt. Then the craftsmen built a door heavy enough to keep out an Indian attack. They made a strong latch and a heavy bar for an extra barricade. Mr. Birkins drilled a hole in the door for the latchstring that would lift the latch from outside. He also made a small peephole.

"You peer out that before you open the door each morning," he advised them. "That way you'll know if Indians are waiting."

The loft was floored with rough boards. A ladder was made so Matt and Becky could climb up to their beds. They would sleep on the cornhusk mattresses Ma was making. Pa hoped to get buffalo skins to keep the children warm.

The men put a plank shelf on the wall to hold Ma's pewter mug and wooden plates. They built a bed into the corner opposite the fire. They made stools and benches and a crude table. Matt whittled pegs so Pa's rifle could hang above the fireplace. Outside, the women and children were helping chink, or fill in, the gaps in the log walls. They packed them tightly with a mixture of moss and mud and sticks.

Now the cabin was complete. It was time for the housewarming, the lighting of the first fire on the hearth. A little wiry old man brought out a fiddle. Everybody ate and sang and danced till sunrise. Ma was very pleased with the cabin. But she still didn't have the furniture she wanted. And she didn't have a window.

Autumn came, and the crops were brought in. Pa took Matt hunting. They didn't find buffalo, but they did kill a

bear. Now they had a good supply of meat and a bearskin to sleep under on winter nights.

"I wish I had my own gun," Matt said. "That way we'd have more chance of finding game."

"Guns are hard to come by," Pa said. "They cost a lot. When you're a man, you'll have one."

Matt was thirteen that winter. He was good at whittling now, and he helped Pa make a cupboard and other things that Ma could use. He helped Pa build a fine table—they worked out in the half-faced camp so Ma wouldn't know. They made the table in pieces, and when Ma was asleep on Christmas Eve, Pa and Matt brought the table in and put it together.

Becky was growing, too. She helped care for their new baby brother, Jason. Pa made a cradle for Jason out of a hollow log. Mrs. Birkins visited, bringing baby clothes.

That summer the Craleys had a fine garden. Matt went hunting often with Pa's rifle. Jake Birkins taught him how to trap. They did so well that by autumn they had furs to trade. Pa had trading goods, too. He and Mr. Birkins decided to go back through the Cumberland Gap to the nearest town. Matt wanted to go, too. But he understood when Pa said he must look after Ma and the young ones.

"I'll leave you the rifle," Pa told him. "Mr. Birkins will be taking his along, because Jake has his own."

One day while Pa was gone, Jake came riding over to get Mrs. Craley. His mother was sick and needed nursing. "Matt will have to look after Becky and Jason while I'm gone," Ma said.

Matt was glad she trusted him. Everything went along smoothly the first two days. On the morning of the third day, Becky ran to open the cabin door. Matt stopped her. "Remember what Mr. Birkins said." Matt peered out the hole. He saw a scarred face, buckskin clothes, black braids. *Indians.* Only one, or more? He couldn't tell.

Matt thought hard. He went to the fireplace on tiptoe, took down Pa's rifle, and loaded it. He whispered to Becky, "Get some food."

28

Then Matt eased the heavy barricade out of its socket. He opened the door a crack. There was only one Indian, a dignified old man. Matt opened the door.

"Welcome," he said, trying to sound like Pa. He held the rifle pointing down, so the Indian could see that it was there but that Matt meant no harm. Matt nodded his head towards Becky. She came forward, carrying a wooden bowl filled with corn-meal pudding. The Indian came inside and sat down solemnly. He tasted the pudding, and then he ate some more. He ate the apples Becky offered him. After a long while, he untied two rabbit skins from his belt and laid them on the floor. He nodded to Matt and left.

Ma turned white when she heard about it. Pa looked proud. "Our children are growing up," he said. After that, Indians came to visit often, but when Ma and Pa were there.

In October, all the nearby families got together to help raise another cabin. Winter was mild that November and December. One day Pa said, "We're going to spend Christmas at the Birkins' cabin."

"Christmas in someone else's home?" Ma exclaimed. But she was glad of the chance to visit friends.

Pa sent the others on ahead a few days early. "I have things to do," he said. They knew he meant Christmas presents.

"What are you men up to this year?" Ma asked, laughing. Matt didn't know.

Ma wrapped baby Jason up in a bearskin to keep him warm. She rode Nellie, and Matt took Becky with him on Blaze. He had Pa's rifle tied to the saddle.

Christmas at the Birkins' meant venison and bear and turkey. It meant games and singing and a lot of giggling by the girls. But no one knew what Pa had been doing. Pa didn't bring anything with him when he came. There were only the gifts Ma had made—new clothes for everyone and a cornhusk doll for Becky. Matt was glad that he had whittled toys for Becky and Jason and a walnut platter for Ma.

On the day after Christmas, the Craleys rode back to their cabin through falling snow. Pa kept urging them to hurry. "Why on earth?" Ma demanded.

"I want to get home before dark," Pa said.

Just before they came to the clearing, Pa spurred Blaze. "I'm going ahead. Matt will look after the rest of you." He disappeared into the forest.

When Matt and the others reached the cabin, smoke was already spiraling from the chimney. A rosy glow tinted the gray sky. Pa threw the door open.

"Come inside. You too, Matt. The animals can wait."

The fire leaped gloriously in the fireplace. The orange flames lit the dark metal of Pa's rifle hanging against the chimney—and *another* rifle. Matt heard himself gasp.

Pa lifted the gun down and put it in Matt's hands. "Every man should have his own rifle," Pa said. "It's time for this now. You've proved that."

Matt ran his hand over the polished maple and brass. He felt like shouting, and he felt like crying. He wasn't going to cry, though, any more than he had when the Indian came.

Ma watched them proudly. Pa grinned at her. "Mrs. Craley, you're looking in the wrong direction. Turn around."

Ma did. She gasped. Becky smiled a big smile. There was a window in the far wall, where it would catch the rays of the morning sun. The twilight came through it dimly now. It was not glass, but something that would let light through all the same. Something covered with elegant fancy writing.

Joshua Lansing Craley
Maria Blacklock Craley
March 15, 1787

"I got the idea when you talked about using oiled parchment," Pa said, smiling. "What better use for our wedding certificate? Merry Christmas, Maria."